This is Albert Le Blanc. Even from the back he looks sad. His head hangs low. His shoulders are hunched. His arms flop loosely by his side.

From the front, Albert Le Blanc looks very sad indeed. He has the saddest eyes you ever saw. Which is strange, because Albert Le Blanc... But wait. Let me tell this story from the very beginning...

This edition produced for The Book People Ltd.,

Hall Wood Avenue, Haydock, St. Helens, WA11 9UL

First published in hardback in Great Britain by HarperCollins Publishers Ltd in 2002
First published in paperback in Great Britain by Collins Picture Books in 2003

1 3 5 7 9 10 8 6 4 2

ISBN: 0-00-776983-0

Collins Picture Books is an imprint of the Children's Division, part of HarperCollins Publishers Ltd.

Text and illustrations copyright © Nick Butterworth 2002, 2003

The author/illustrator asserts the moral right to be identified as the author/illustrator of the work.
A CIP catalogue record for this title is available from the British Library.

The HarperCollins website address is: www.harpercollinschildrensbooks.co.uk

Printed in Thailand

Albert Le Blanc

Nick Butterworth

Collins

An imprint of HarperCollins*Publishers*

When Albert Le Blanc first appeared, sitting all by himself in Mr Jolly's toy shop, the other toys could only stare. He did look so sad.

"Poor love," said Sally the hippo. "We must try and cheer him up."

"You could do your funny dancing," said Toby the cat. "That would make him laugh."

"My dancing is not funny," said Sally. "It is beautiful and artistic." The other toys looked at each other and tried not to smile.

"I know a joke," said a little mouse called Pickle. "But I can't remember the funny bit at the end."

Everyone agreed that this could make the joke a lot less funny. It might even make it Not Funny At All. Pickle flopped down and stared at the floor.

It was then that Jack-in-a-box (who at that moment was not in his box) had an idea.

"Why don't we all try very hard to think of something happy and funny. Something to cheer up a very sad bear. Then, we could put all our things together. . .

and make a show!"

It was a good idea. Everybody thought so. At first, the toys sat quietly thinking. What could they say? What could they do? Something happy. Something funny.

Maurice, the steam engine, let off a little steam as he tried to think. Lizzie, the humming top, hummed to herself as she thought. Hmmmmmmm . . .

"I've remembered my joke!" squeaked Pickle, suddenly.

"Sssh! dear," said Sally. "I'm getting an idea."

All at once, it seemed that the other toys were getting ideas too.

Toby began to snigger and Jack-in-a-box started to chuckle. Sally began to titter and went off to borrow a hat and to find some face paints.

Albert Le Blanc watched, from where he was sitting, as the toys became very busy. What was going on? What were they up to?

Albert Le Blanc did not have to wait very long to find out. Sally was the first to introduce herself.

"Good evening!" she said with a bow. "I am Sally. Hippopotamus and Ballerina. This evening, we, the toys of Mr Jolly's toy shop, will present a Happy and Entertaining Treat, especially to Cheer, Amuse and Tickle the Funny Bone of a Very Sad Bear."

Albert Le Blanc looked puzzled.

"I am very pleased to meet you," he said. "My name is Albert. Albert Le Blanc. I am from France. But, please, let me say. . . you must not think that I am. . . ." But Albert Le Blanc was not allowed to say.

"Silence, please, for Miss Pickle!" the hippopotamus boomed loudly.
Pickle came and stood nervously in front of the large, sad-looking bear. She shuffled her feet and cleared her throat.
But no words came. Whatever Pickle had remembered earlier, she had suddenly forgotten again.
"I can't remember my joke..." she said and she flopped down again and stared at the floor.

"Never mind," said Albert, kindly. "I am sure
it was very funny. And you really must not
think that I am. . ."

But at that moment, with a twang and a zing, Jack-in-a-box sprang out of his box. He bounced up and down in front of Albert Le Blanc and as he did, he began to sing.

"I bounce. . .with a BOING!
I bounce. . .with a POING!
And while. . .I am bouncing,
I'm singing. . .this SOING!"

"Be careful dear," said Sally. But Jack was enjoying himself. He bounced even higher.

"I like. . .to bounce HIGH!
As high. . .as the SKY!
Sometimes. . .when I'm bouncing,
I'm sure. . .I could FL. . ."

THUMP!

Poor Jack. He bounced so high, he bumped his head on a shelf. He fell in a tangled heap in front of Albert.

"Slight technical problem," mumbled Jack as he tried to untie the knot which he had accidentally tied in his long body.

Albert hid his face in his paws.

"Please do not worry," he said. "You really, really, must not think that I am . . ."

Once again, Sally did not
let him finish. To Albert's
amazement, she leapt out in
front of him, wearing a yellow
pointed hat and a big, red,
face-painted smile.

Of course, Sally did mean to
be funny. But she didn't mean
to slip. Or slide. And she most
certainly didn't mean to crash
into Albert Le Blanc. But that
is just what Sally did.

Together, the bear and the hippopotamus landed in a confused heap. From underneath Sally, Albert Le Blanc let out a great roar.

"**P**LEASE!" he shouted. "I keep trying
to tell you! I AM NOT UN-HAPPY!"
There was silence. As Sally and Albert
struggled to get up, Albert went on.
"I am not sad at all. It is just the way I am
made. I just happen to have a sad look
on my face."

"Oh no you don't!" interrupted Toby the cat. "Not any more!"

Suddenly everyone saw that Albert Le Blanc was wearing a great, big, red smile! It was Sally's smile. The toys began to giggle.

"Oh! Silly me," said Sally. "I'm so sorry. I must have kissed you by mistake!"

The toys giggled even more and some of them laughed out loud.

But now, what was happening to Albert Le Blanc?

He began to shake and he grabbed hold of his tummy. His shoulders started to heave up and down. His nose wrinkled up and his sad eyes almost disappeared.

Then, to everyone's great surprise, Albert Le Blanc roared out the funniest and the loudest laugh any of the toys had ever heard.

"H-HEE! H-HEE! H-HEE!"

Albert's enormous laugh made everyone else laugh even more.

"H-HEE! H-HEE! H-HEE! H-HEE!"

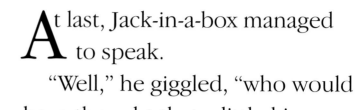

At last, Jack-in-a-box managed to speak.

"Well," he giggled, "who would have thought that a little kiss could put such a big smile on someone's face!"

Everybody laughed again. But the biggest, deepest, loudest *and the funniest* laugh of all, came from a sad-looking bear called. . .

Albert Le Blanc.

A big thank you!

Some familiar faces make guest appearances in this book with the permission of:

Mick Inkpen, for Kipper; Chorion plc, for Noddy;
Martin Handford, for Where's Wally?; Jane Hissey, for Old Bear and Little Bear;
David McKee, for Elmer; Michael Bond, for Paddington;
Raymond Briggs, for The Snowman; HIT Entertainment plc, for Bob the Builder.
Percy the Park Keeper's friend, the fox, appeared without anyone's permission.
Q Pootle 5 just appeared out of the blue.